W9-CUC-950

Ride On

FAITH ERIN HICKS

Colors by KELLY FITZPATRICK

First Second
NEW YORK

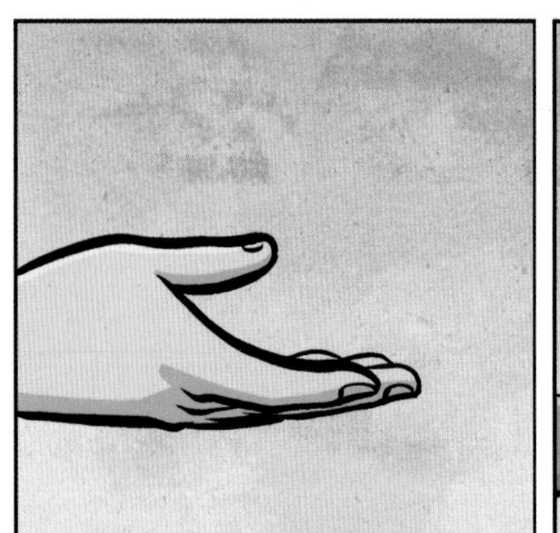

SNRF

SNF

SO GLAD SUMMER'S OVER. SO GLAD!

A NEW GIRL? CLAUDIA DIDN'T SAY ANYONE NEW WAS RIDING TODAY.
WHO'S SHE ON?

QUINN.

HMMMM.

SHE'S A GOOD RIDER.
SHE'S A GREAT RIDER.

WHO *IS* SHE??

SAM!!
NICE TO SEE YOU TOO ON THIS FINE SATURDAY MORNING, NORRIE.
SAM! YOU ARE THE *ONLY BOY* AT EDGEWOOD STABLES!!
WOW, NORRIE, YOU'RE RIGHT, I AM.
HOW COULD I FORGET, SINCE YOU REMIND ME EVERY TWENTY MINUTES.

AS THE ONLY BOY, YOU GOTTA ASK THIS NEW RIDER WHO SHE IS! ALSO FIND OUT WHAT SHE'S DOING HERE.
WHY DOES ME BEING THE ONLY BOY MEAN I HAVE TO BE THE EDGEWOOD STABLES WELCOMING COMMITTEE?

NO TIME FOR QUESTIONS! THIS IS YOUR MISSION, WHICH YOU MUST ACCEPT!
THAT'S NOT HOW THAT GOES. IT'S "YOUR MISSION, SHOULD YOU CHOOSE TO ACCEPT—"
WAIT, I KNOW HER.

YOU DO?
YEAH.

I SAW HER AT THE WAVERLY STABLES SCHOOLING SHOW LAST FALL.

SHE WAS A GOOD RIDER THEN TOO. I THINK HER NAME'S VICTORIA.

WAVERLY STABLES??
NORRIE...

OUR RIVAL!
THEY AREN'T OUR RIVAL, NORRIE. THEY'RE JUST ANOTHER RIDING STABLE.

OUR SWORN ENEMY IN ALL THINGS HORSE RELATED!
THEY DON'T EVEN KNOW WE EXIST.

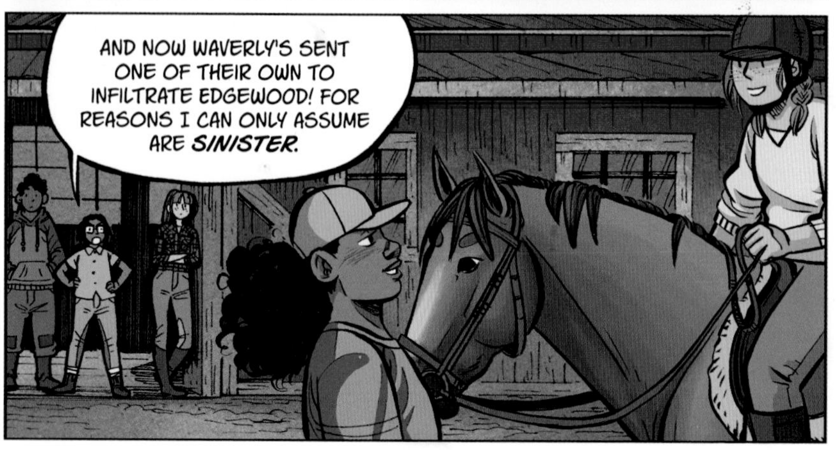
AND NOW WAVERLY'S SENT ONE OF THEIR OWN TO INFILTRATE EDGEWOOD! FOR REASONS I CAN ONLY ASSUME ARE SINISTER.

WELL,
WE'LL JUST
SEE ABOUT THAT,
WON'T WE?

I'M GONNA
GO. THESE
STALLS AREN'T
GOING TO MUCK
THEMSELVES.
HAVE
FUN GLARING
INTO SPACE,
NORRIE.
THANK YOU.
I WILL.

I SHOULD GIVE HER A CHANCE. I SHOULDN'T REJECT HER JUST BECAUSE SHE'S FROM WAVERLY.

I'LL GIVE HER THE OLD EDGEWOOD WELCOME.

WHA—

HI, I'M NORRIE! I SAW YOU HAVING A LESSON WITH CLAUDIA. SHE'S THE BARN MANAGER HERE AT EDGEWOOD, AND I HELP HER OUT WITH THE STABLE STUFF.
SO I GUESS YOU COULD SAY I'M KINDA THE *ASSISTANT* BARN MANAGER, HAHAHA!

I HOPE YOU HAD FUN RIDING QUINN. SHE'S REALLY GOOD WITH THE YOUNGER RIDERS. SHE'S BEEN AT EDGEWOOD AS LONG AS I HAVE.
SNRF
WE JUST FINISHED UP ALL OUR SUMMER RIDING CAMP PROGRAMS. I HELPED OUT WITH THOSE TOO.

MY FRIENDS HAZEL AND SAM HELP OUT AROUND EDGEWOOD TOO. SAM'S THE ONLY BOY WHO RIDES HERE, SO IT'S FUN TO BUG HIM ABOUT THAT. HAZEL'S KINDA…WELL, YOU'LL SEE. SHE'S AWESOME, BUT SHE DOESN'T TALK MUCH.

I GUESS THAT'S WHY ME AND HER ARE SUCH GOOD FRIENDS: I TALK ENOUGH FOR TWO PEOPLE.

OR, LIKE, TWO *DOZEN* PEOPLE, HAHAHA!

HEY, UM—
NORRIE. UNOFFICIAL EDGEWOOD STABLES ASSISTANT BARN MANAGER.

YEAH. LOOK. I JUST WANT TO GET THIS HORSE GROOMED AND BACK IN HER STALL, OKAY?
SURE! *TOTALLY* UNDERSTAND.

PAT PAT

HORSES ARE THE BEST, AREN'T THEY?

YOU KNOW YOU'RE THE BEST, DON'T YOU, QUINNY? SMOOCHIE!

HMM DE DUM DUM

I'M JUST HERE TO RIDE. I'M NOT LOOKING TO MAKE FRIENDS.

SO DO YOU MIND LEAVING ME ***ALONE*** SO I CAN BRUSH THIS HORSE?

FWIP

TURN!

WHERE'S HAZEL?? THAT NEW GIRL FROM WAVERLY STABLES IS *AWFUL!*

SHE'S AWFUL? WHAT'D SHE DO?
I TRIED TO BE NICE TO HER, SAM, I REALLY DID! EVEN THOUGH SHE'S FROM WAVERLY, I WANTED TO GIVE HER THE BENEFIT OF THE DOUBT.

BOY, WAS I *WRONG.*
SHE COMPLETELY REJECTED MY EDGEWOOD STABLES WELCOME.

MAYBE SHE'S JUST SHY—
THIS IS JUST THE KIND OF COLDHEARTED REACTION I'D EXPECT FROM A WAVERLY STABLES RIDER. OUR GREATEST RIVAL!

OUR GREATEST RIVAL WHO DOESN'T EVEN KNOW WE EXIST.
I NEED TO TELL HAZEL.

ELOUISE, *WHAT* ARE YOU DOING?
PRACTICING YE OLDE HEADSTANDS, VIC. I GOT A JOB AT THAT RENAISSANCE FAIR ON GRANVILLE ROAD THROUGH THE END OF OCTOBER. PAYS FIFTEEN BUCKS AN HOUR.
I'M A JESTER.

YEAH, BUT ... DO YOU HAVE TO PRACTICE OUTSIDE ON THE LAWN?
THE CEILING'S TOO LOW IN THE LIVING ROOM.

ARE THOSE YOUR RIDING BOOTS?

YEAH, THEY ARE.
DOES THAT MEAN YOU WENT *RIDING??*
WHUMP
PLEASE DON'T MAKE A BIG DEAL ABOUT IT.

VICTORIA, MY ONE AND ONLY SISTER, WHEN DO I MAKE A BIG DEAL ABOUT *ANYTHING??*
IS THIS A TRICK QUESTION? HAVE YOU MET YOU?

SO *SOMETIMES* MAKING A BIG DEAL OVER THINGS IS ON BRAND FOR ME—
I TAKE ISSUE WITH THE "SOMETIMES."

BUT VIC ... YOU'RE RIDING AGAIN. ISN'T THIS A BIG DEAL?

KLACK

NO, IT ISN'T.

THMP
THMP

SIGH.

FWUMP!

Vic

Vic

I'm glad you're riding again
ELOUISE

THREE MONTHS AGO
Waverly Stables

GOOD WORK, VICTORIA. SOFTEN YOUR HANDS JUST A LITTLE.
SEE IF YOU CAN REALLY GET HIM COLLECTED UNDER YOU.

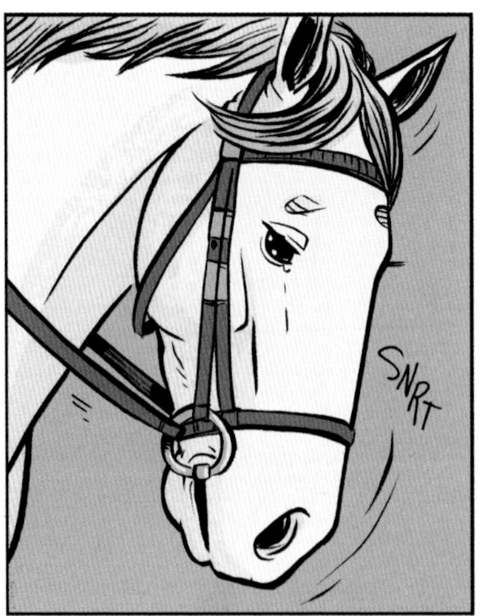
SNRT

VERY NICE.

WHAT'S IT FEEL LIKE TO GET A COMPLIMENT FROM MR. ROSEN?
IT'S SO WEIRD—IT'S NEVER HAPPENED BEFORE! HE NEVER SAYS *ANYTHING* POSITIVE ABOUT MY RIDING.

HE'S TEACHING AN EVENING CLINIC NEXT WEEK. YOU SHOULD COME.
C'MON, TAYLOR, YOU KNOW I CAN'T AFFORD THOSE.

MY MOM CAN BARELY PAY FOR THE WEEKLY LESSONS AS IT IS.
YOU COULD DO SOME WORK AROUND THE BARN TO PAY FOR THE CLINIC. THEY ALWAYS NEED HELP HERE.

NAH, IT'S FINE. I DON'T NEED TO PAY MONEY SO MR. ROSEN CAN TELL ME MY JUMPING FORM SUCKS.
BUT YOU WANT TO COMPETE WITH ME IN THE TRILLIUM CIRCUIT THIS SUMMER, RIGHT? YOU NEED THE CLINICS IF YOU WANT TO WIN ANY RIBBONS.

YEAH, ABOUT THAT...

I KNOW WE'VE BEEN WORKING TOWARD SHOWING TOGETHER THIS SUMMER, BUT I'VE DECIDED NOT TO. I'D RATHER JUST SPEND THAT TIME HANGING OUT WITH THE HORSES.

OH.
YEAH, SURE.

I'M REALLY SORRY. BUT YOU GET IT, RIGHT? I WANT TO RELAX A BIT THIS SUMMER.

ARE YOU...UM, UPSET?

NO, IT'S FINE. I'LL JUST MISS YOU. IT'S NOT AS FUN GOING TO SHOWS WITHOUT YOU.

WE'LL STILL SEE EACH OTHER ALL THE TIME AT WAVERLY. IT'S OUR HOME AWAY FROM HOME.

VICTORIA, I'VE GOT SOMETHING TO TELL YOU.
YEAH?
MY PARENTS BOUGHT ME A HORSE.

WEHHHH, I DON'T WANNA STUDY.
WELL, YOU GOTTA.

HAZEL, HOW CAN YOU DO SCHOOLWORK AT A TIME LIKE THIS? THERE'S A NEW SCHOOLING HORSE COMING TO EDGEWOOD *THIS AFTERNOON!* AREN'T YOU EXCITED?
SURE, BUT THE NEW HORSE WILL STILL BE THERE THIS WEEKEND.

BUT I DON'T *WANT* TO WAIT UNTIL THE WEEKEND. I WANT TO GO TO EDGEWOOD *NOW!*
THIS WAS THE DEAL WITH YOUR PARENTS: SCHOOL NIGHTS ARE FOR STUDYING UNTIL YOU BRING YOUR GRADES UP.

READ
WHUMP

GRADES ARE POOP.
YEAH, THEY ARE.

READ
THIS IS ALL TAHIR'S FAULT.
YOUR BROTHER? WHY'S IT HIS FAULT?

BECAUSE HE'S SO GOOD AT SCHOOL! HE GETS A'S IN *EVERYTHING*.
HE GAVE MY PARENTS UNREALISTIC EXPECTATIONS THAT ALL THEIR KIDS WOULD BE SUPERSMART OVERACHIEVERS.
BOOKS!

HE'LL PROBABLY GROW UP TO SOLVE WORLD HUNGER. THEN MY PARENTS'LL BE, LIKE, "LOOK HOW SMART TAHIR IS, NOREEN. WHEN WILL *YOU* WIN A NOBEL PRIZE?"

UGGGGHHH.
THERE, THERE.
PAT PAT

HOW *DARE* YOU MOCK MY PAIN.
WHAT, ME? YOUR BEST FRIEND? I WOULD NEVER.

READ
24

HEY, CHECK IT OUT.
NUDGE
BIOLOGY

RETURNS

THAT WAVERLY STABLES MEAN GIRL GOES TO SCHOOL HERE?
YEAH, I THINK SO. I'D SEE HER AROUND NOW AND THEN.

AND YOU NEVER TOLD ME??
WHY WOULD I? SHE'S JUST ANOTHER STUDENT.
WHO USED TO RIDE AT *OUR RIVAL STABLE!* AND NOW RIDES AT ***EDGEWOOD.***

VICTORIA!

HEY, ASH.
WHERE'VE YOU BEEN? WE HAD OUR FIRST YEARBOOK MEETING LAST WEEK AND YOU WEREN'T THERE.

YEAH, I GUESS I'VE JUST BEEN REALLY BUSY.

SERIOUSLY? BUT WE'VE ALWAYS WORKED TOGETHER ON YEARBOOK. YOU, ME, TAYLOR, SARAH, AND OTHER SARAH. THE WAVERLY CREW.
READ
READ
YEAH, IT SUCKS, BUT I'M JUST KINDA SWAMPED AND HOMEWORK AND... UM, YOU KNOW.

AW, MAN, WE'RE GONNA MISS YOU.
ME TOO.

I'LL SEE YOU AROUND, OKAY?
YEAH. SEE YOU.

OOOH, *DRAMA!* IT'S THE *BEST!*
BIOLOGY

RETU
NORRIE, WE NEED TO STUDY.
IT'S SO MYSTERIOUS.

IF YOU COULD JUST FOCUS YOUR BRAIN ON BIOLOGY—
WHY WOULD THAT WAVERLY MEAN GIRL MAKE A LAME EXCUSE TO NOT HANG OUT WITH HER FRIENDS? I MUST DISCOVER THE REASON WHY.

AND WHY IS SHE SUDDENLY TAKING RIDING LESSONS AT WAVERLY'S RIVAL STABLE, EDGEWOOD?
I REALLY DON'T THINK THEY KNOW WE EXIST.

IN HER FIRST VISIT TO EDGEWOOD, THIS GIRL CREATED PURE CHAOS! BUT THE QUESTION REMAINS, *WHY?*
SHE DIDN'T CREATE CHAOS, SHE JUST HAD A RIDING LESSON.

WHAT SINISTER MOTIVES DOES SHE HAVE? THE GAME'S AFOOT, WATSON!
EVEN SHERLOCK HOLMES DID HIS HOMEWORK.

NOREEN, GET DOWN FROM THAT TABLE AT ONCE.

SORRY, MS. GREEN.

EDGEWOOD
STABLE

THMP
THNK

HEY, BUDDY.
YOU NEW HERE
TOO?

SNORT!

NEEIIIGHH

VICTORIA, ISN'T IT? CLAUDIA'S BEEN TELLING ME ABOUT YOU.

I'M MS. ANDERSON, BUT ALL THE KIDS CALL ME MS. A. I OWN EDGEWOOD STABLES.
NICE TO MEET YOU.

I KNOW YOU'VE MET CLAUDIA ALREADY. SHE MANAGES THE BARN AND TEACHES LESSONS.
I COULDN'T RUN THIS PLACE WITHOUT HER.

CLAUDIA SAYS YOU'RE QUITE THE RIDER.
THANKS. I'M GLAD SHE THINKS SO.

I DO THINK SO.
I TRUST CLAUDIA WITH A LOT. MY BARN, MY HORSES, MY YOUNG RIDERS. WHEN SHE SAYS THERE'S A PROMISING NEW RIDER AT EDGEWOOD, I TAKE NOTE.

SEE THAT HANDSOME YOUNG GELDING TEARING UP THE PADDOCK?

SNORT!

YES.

HIS NAME IS WINTER. I JUST BOUGHT HIM, HOPING TO TURN HIM INTO A LESSON HORSE. BUT HE'S A BIT... *SPICY.*
KATHNK
KATHNK
KATHUNK

HE NEEDS A PATIENT AND TALENTED RIDER TO TEACH HIM TO BE A LITTLE CALMER. TAKE THE EDGES OFF HIM.

I WAS THINKING THAT RIDER MIGHT BE YOU.

THANKS FOR DRIVING US TO THE STABLE, TAHIR.
NO PROBLEM. ALTHOUGH IT DOES MAKE ME FEEL LIKE A CHAUFFEUR WHEN YOU GUYS SIT IN THE BACK LIKE THAT.

MOM SAYS YOU GOTTA BE HOME FOR SUPPER, NORRIE. YOU CAN'T STAY HERE UNTIL LATE LIKE YOU USUALLY DO.
UGH, I *KNOW.*

I'LL PICK YOU UP AT FIVE.
YEAH, YEAH.
BYE, TAHIR.

STOP MAKING GOOGLY EYES AT MY BROTHER.
I CAN'T HELP IT. HE'S JUST SO... ***SPARKLY.***

YEAH, HE'S A PRINCE.

I CAN'T WAIT TO CHECK OUT THE NEW HORSE. IT'S BEEN ***FOREVER*** SINCE WE HAD ANYONE NEW.

GOOD MORNING ROCKET, NUTMEG, QUINN. DON'T WORRY, I STILL LOVE YOU ALL.

BUT A *NEW HORSE!* IT'S JUST SO—

—EXCITING—

WHY IS THAT NEW GIRL ON OUR NEW HORSE???
I'D SAY SHE'S GETTING A LESSON FROM CLAUDIA.

I AM SO UPSET RIGHT NOW.

NORRIE, HAZEL, I'M GLAD YOU'RE BOTH HERE SO EARLY.
MS. A—

HAVE YOU TWO MET VICTORIA? SHE STARTED RIDING HERE LAST WEEK.
YEAH, WE'VE MET.

WONDERFUL. I'VE PUT HER IN CHARGE OF TRAINING OUR NEW SCHOOLING HORSE. THEY GET ON REALLY WELL, DON'T YOU THINK?
WAIT, WHAT?

THE NEW HORSE. VICTORIA'S GOING TO BE WORKING WITH HIM FOR THE NEXT FEW MONTHS.

AS THE UNOFFICIAL ASSISTANT BARN MANAGER, I'M SURE YOU'LL DO EVERYTHING YOU CAN TO HELP HER OUT.
UM, YEAH, OKAY.

I KNOW ALL OF YOU WILL DO AN AMAZING JOB PREPARING WINTER FOR HIS NEW CAREER AS A SCHOOLING HORSE.

FWIP

HOW DARE SHE.

LICK
SNRF

haha
SNRF

YOU.

ME?
YOU...YOU... ***INTRUDER*** FROM ANOTHER STABLE!

I... WHAT?

I TRIED TO BE NICE TO YOU! I GAVE YOU AN EDGEWOOD STABLES WELCOME, BUT YOU THREW IT BACK IN MY FACE!

LOOK, I'M HERE TO RIDE, THAT'S IT. I'M NOT INTO HANGING AROUND THE BARN AND MAKING FRIENDS WITH THE OTHER GIRLS HERE.
I DON'T SEE WHAT THE PROBLEM IS.

I'LL TELL YOU WHAT THE PROBLEM IS. I'VE RIDDEN AT EDGEWOOD SINCE I WAS SEVEN YEARS OLD. I SPEND EVERY FREE MINUTE HERE. I MUCK THE STALLS, FEED THE HORSES, I HELP CLAUDIA TEACH LESSONS.

EDGEWOOD IS MY ***HOME.*** AND YOU MADE ME FEEL ***WEIRD.***

WELL, THAT'S NOT MY PROBLEM—
IT ***IS*** YOUR PROBLEM. BECAUSE NOW I'M GOING TO SHUN YOU.

YOU'RE GOING TO SHUN ME? ARE YOU AMISH OR SOMETHING?
NO, BUT I'M STILL GONNA DO IT!

LET THE SHUNNING COMMENCE!

FWAAA!

JUST SO I KNOW, BEING SHUNNED MEANS YOU'RE GONNA LET ME RIDE IN PEACE, RIGHT?

SHUNN!
WSST

GREAT! THAT'S EXACTLY WHAT I WANTED.

FWUMP

WANT ME TO TACK UP ROCKET FOR YOU?
NO, I'LL DO IT.

THREE MONTHS AGO

HAHA!

I'M SO HAPPY FOR YOU, TAYLOR!

WHAT CHANGED THEIR MIND?
SNRF
IT WAS ALL THE RIBBONS I WON DURING THE LAST SHOW SEASON. THAT FINALLY CONVINCED THEM THAT RIDING IS REALLY IMPORTANT TO ME.

AND THAT IT'S SOMETHING I WANT TO DO FOREVER. I'M GOING TO COMPETE AT THE GOLD LEVEL IN A COUPLE YEARS. MAYBE THE OLYMPICS SOMEDAY.

I'M SO HAPPY FOR YOU.

YEAH, YOU SAID THAT ALREADY.
BUT I AM. I MEAN, HOW LONG HAVE WE BEEN RIDING TOGETHER AT WAVERLY? SINCE WE WERE SIX YEARS OLD?

I REMEMBER THOSE BEGINNER LEAD LINE CLASSES. I ALWAYS RODE THAT REALLY FAT PONY, WHAT WAS HER NAME—
DAISY. SHE WAS SO ROUND! I'D PRACTICALLY ROLL RIGHT OFF HER BACK.

DAISY, RIGHT.
AND NOW I FINALLY HAVE A HORSE OF MY OWN.

WE'RE SO HAPPY FOR TAYLOR, AREN'T WE—
VICTORIA, WHEN DID YOU STOP WANTING YOUR OWN HORSE?

WHAT? YOU KNOW I'D LOVE MY OWN HORSE, BUT MY MOM'S AN ACCOUNTANT. SHE'S NEVER GOING TO BE ABLE TO BUY ME ONE.
YOU DIDN'T CARE ABOUT THAT LAST YEAR. WE TALKED ABOUT IT A LOT: WE WERE GOING TO HAVE OUR OWN HORSES SOMEDAY, ***BOTH*** OF US.

I KNOW, BUT...I STARTED FEELING BAD WHENEVER I ASKED MY MOM. I KNEW WHAT HER ANSWER WOULD BE.

AND I GUESS I FELT LIKE I HAD TO ACCEPT IT.

YOU DON'T RIDE AS MUCH AS YOU DID LAST YEAR, EITHER.

TAYLOR, I'M AT WAVERLY ***ALL THE TIME.***

YOU'RE HERE HANGING OUT! YOU RIDE, BUT YOU'RE NOT ***PRACTICING.***

YOU AREN'T TRYING TO GET ***BETTER.***

SO? I'M A GOOD ENOUGH RIDER. WHY DO I NEED TO BE ***BETTER?***
SO YOU CAN COMPETE IN SHOWS WITH ME.

BUT I JUST *TOLD* YOU—
IT'S FINE. WHATEVER.

UM, WHEN IS YOUR HORSE ARRIVING AT WAVERLY?

NEXT WEEK. HIS NAME IS KING.

I CAN'T WAIT TO MEET HIM.

AW, YOU DON'T HAVE THE MATCHA SOFT SERVE ANYMORE?
SORRY, IT WAS A SEASONAL FLAVOR.

NOOOO, WHYYY, MATCHAAA.
THERE ARE OTHER FLAVORS, NORRIE.

BUT GREEN TEA IS THE MOST DELICIOUS SOFT SERVE FLAVOR! IT'S A SCIENTIFIC *FACT.*
VANILLA, PLEASE.
CHOCOLATE
VANILLA

WHY'D YOU GET A VANILLA WHEN THEY HAD VANILLA-CHOCOLATE SWIRL?
DON'T SHAME MY ICE CREAM CHOICES.

Chocolate Shop
BUS STOP
BEYOND THE GALAXY
BUT IT'S SCIENTIFIC FACT IF YOU CAN'T HAVE MATCHA SOFT SERVE, THE BEST ALTERNATIVE IS VANILLA-CHOCOLATE SWIRL.
NO, IT ISN'T.

LOOK, I'M JUST TRYING TO SAVE YOU FROM BLAND ICE CREAM CHOICES—
GUYS, *WAIT. WAIT WAIT WAIT.*

LOOK!
LOOK AT IT!

BEYOND THE GALAXY
IT'S SO BEAUTIFUL!

A MONTH UNTIL THE NEW *BEYOND THE GALAXY* SEASON STARTS! GUYS, I'VE BEEN WAITING YEARS FOR THIS!
I'M EXCITED FOR THE REBOOT TOO.

THIS ISN'T A ***REBOOT!*** IT'S A ***CONTINUATION*** OF THE GREATEST SCIENCE FICTION TV SHOW EVER MADE! A SHOW CRUELLY CUT DOWN IN ITS PRIME!

FINALLY THE CLIFF-HANGER AT THE END OF SEASON THREE WILL BE RESOLVED!
WE'LL FIND OUT WHAT HAPPENED TO CAPTAIN FINN AND FIRST OFFICER JOSEFINA AT THE ASSEMBLY OF UNITED PLANETS, WHEN THEY TRIED TO PREVENT AN ALL-OUT GALACTIC WAR!
HOW ARE YOU THE CHILLEST PERSON EVER AT EDGEWOOD BUT YOU GO BONKERS WHENEVER THIS SHOW COMES UP?

I CAN'T BELIEVE *BEYOND THE GALAXY* IS ACTUALLY COMING BACK. I'VE MISSED YOU SO MUCH, INTREPID CREW OF THE USS *STARCRAFT VIGILANCE*.

YOU KNOW WHAT WE SHOULD DO? LET'S DRESS UP FOR THE SHOW PREMIERE. I REALLY LIKE THAT BLUE ALIEN LADY.
LIEUTENANT NEKO?

YEAH, SHE WAS SO COOL. I LOVED HOW SHE COULD DO, LIKE, ALIEN JUDO.

SAM! WHAT'RE YOU HUGGING THAT BUS SHELTER FOR?

OH, YOU KNOW, JUST... UH, YOU KNOW.
OOH, MILKSHAKE. GIMMEE.

HEY!
CALM DOWN, LITTLE BRO. JUST TAKING A SIP.
SO WHO'S THIS?

THESE ARE MY FRIENDS NORRIE AND HAZEL.
NORRIE AND HAZEL, THESE ARE MY BROTHERS, LAURENCE AND CALEB.
HI.
HEY.

?
?

JUST *FRIENDS,* HUH?
YES. JUST FRIENDS.

HA! YEAH, I SEE HOW IT IS.

WINK

SEE YOU LATER, SAM! HAVE FUN HANGING OUT WITH YOUR GIRLFRIENDS!
OOPS, I MEAN YOUR *"JUST FRIENDS"*!

WHAT JUST HAPPENED?
UGGGGH.

SERIOUSLY, WHAT WAS THAT?
IT'S JUST HOW MY BROTHERS ARE! GIRLS ARE NEVER JUST ***FRIENDS,*** THEY'RE ONLY ***GIRLFRIENDS.***

IT DRIVES ME ***CRAZY.***

MY DAD'S THE SAME WAY! HE'S ALWAYS, LIKE, "SAMUEL, YOU RIDE AT THAT STABLE WITH *ALL* THOSE GIRLS, SURELY *ONE* OF THEM IS YOUR GIRLFRIEND?"
UH... IS ONE?

NO! I JUST LIKE RIDING! AND THERE HAPPENS TO BE LOTS OF GIRLS AT EDGEWOOD, THAT'S *ALL!*

SORRY, SAM.
WHATEVER. LET'S TALK ABOUT *BEYOND THE GALAXY.*

I'M UP FOR COSPLAYING. I WANNA BE THE ALIEN LADY WITH ANTENNAE.

HER NAME IS ENSIGN SI AND THEY'RE NOT ANTENNA, THEY'RE EXTRASENSORY FEELERS.

GROCERY

YEAH, I LIKE HER FEELERS.

SNORT!

GOOD BOY.

NNNEEEEIIII

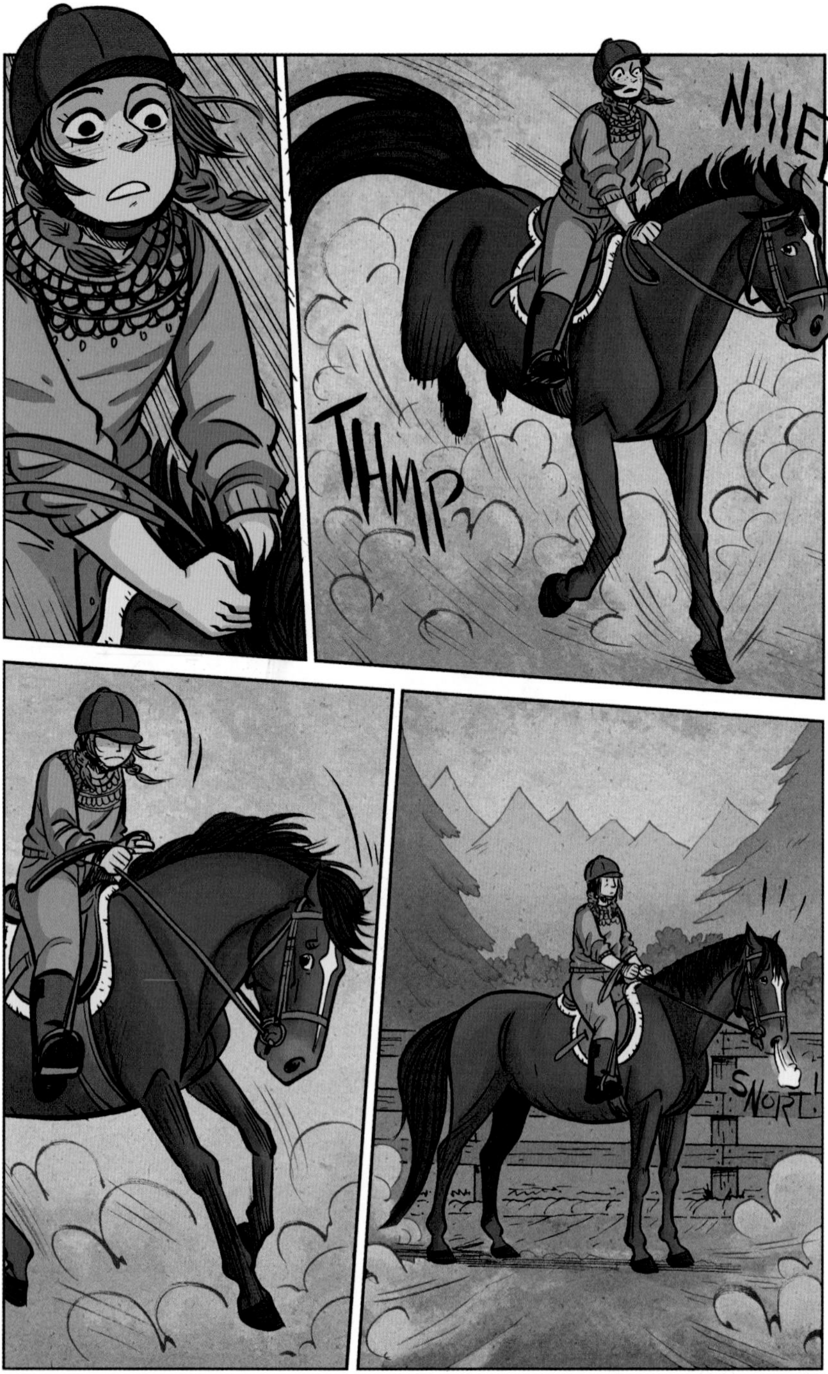

NIIIEEGHH
THMP

SNORT!

HFFFF

YOU OKAY?

YEAH, I'M GOOD.
MAYBE JUST WALK HIM FOR A BIT, CALM HIM DOWN.

SURE THING.

DID NORRIE GIVE YOU HER TRADITIONAL "WELCOME TO EDGEWOOD" ALREADY?
HA, YEAH. SHE DID.

SHARING A PLACE WITH OTHER HORSE-CRAZY GIRLS WAS ALWAYS MY FAVORITE PART OF RIDING WHEN I WAS YOUNGER.

THERE WAS SOMETHING SPECIAL ABOUT MY HORSE FRIENDS.

TOO BAD THEY ALL GREW OUT OF RIDING AND I'M STILL HERE.
STILL STUCK ON HORSES. AH WELL.

BGT

BGT

UM...IS THAT A *BEYOND THE GALAXY* PATCH ON YOUR BAG?

YEAH, IT IS. DO YOU LIKE THE SHOW?

YEAH.
MEOW

Lt. NEKO
BEYOND THE GALAXY
COMIX

BEYOND THE GALAXY
I REALLY LIKED *BEYOND THE GALAXY* WHEN I WAS A KID. BUT I DIDN'T HAVE ANY FRIENDS WHO WERE INTO IT.

FOR REAL? EVERYONE I KNEW LOVED IT.
MY BROTHERS AND I WOULD WATCH RERUNS ON CABLE AND HALF THE NEIGHBORHOOD KIDS WOULD COME OVER TO WATCH WITH US.

I GUESS MY FRIENDS WERE ALL GIRLS WHO RODE HORSES, NOT BOYS WHO WATCHED OLD SCIENCE FICTION TV SHOWS.
LOTS OF GIRLS LIKE *BTG*. NORRIE AND HAZEL LIKE IT.
NOT AS MUCH AS I DO, BUT STILL.

WE'RE ALL PLANNING TO DRESS UP AS CHARACTERS FROM THE SHOW WHEN THE NEW SEASON STARTS UP NEXT MONTH—
THERE'S A NEW *BEYOND THE GALAXY* SHOW?

YEAH, IT'S A CONTINUATION OF SEASON THREE AFTER THE SHOW WAS CANCELED. THEY'RE BRINGING BACK THE ORIGINAL ACTORS EVEN THOUGH IT'S BEEN EIGHTEEN YEARS BETWEEN SEASONS.
I'VE NEVER ACTUALLY WATCHED THE FINAL EPISODE OF SEASON THREE.

I HEARD THE SHOW WAS CANCELED BEFORE I FINISHED SEASON THREE AND COULDN'T BRING MYSELF TO FINISH IT.

I GET THAT. IF YOU DON'T WATCH IT, YOU WON'T BE TRAUMATIZED BY A CLIFF-HANGER THAT'LL NEVER BE RESOLVED, LIKE I WAS.

PLUS, THE SECOND-TO-LAST EPISODE IS ABOUT ENSIGN SI'S HOMEWORLD, AND THAT'S A GREAT EPISODE.
SO I STOPPED THERE.

IF YOU WANTED, YOU COULD WATCH THE NEW SEASON WITH US. YOU DON'T HAVE TO DRESS UP OR ANYTHING.
OH, THAT WOULD BE—

ACTUALLY, I CAN'T.
REALLY?

YEAH, I...SORRY. BUT THANKS ANYWAY.

OKAY. IT'S NO BIG.

SAM!
WHAT IS IT, NORRIE?

WERE YOU TALKING TO THAT WAVERLY MEAN GIRL?? WE AGREED TO SHUN HER!
NO, *YOU* DECIDED TO SHUN HER, AND THEN BRIBED HAZEL AND ME WITH ICE CREAM SO WE WOULD TOO.

AND YOU'D BETTER GIVE ME THAT MILKSHAKE BACK! WE HAD A DEAL!
NORRIE, IT DOESN'T *MATTER.*

SHE TURNED ME DOWN. SHE DOESN'T WANT TO BE HORSE FRIENDS. SHE DOESN'T WANT TO BE *BTG* FRIENDS.

SHE DOESN'T WANT TO BE ANY KIND OF FRIEND. JUST IGNORE HER.

FINE,
I WILL!

WHO NEEDS
TO KNOW WHO
THAT GIRL IS OR
WHY SHE'S INVADING
MY STABLE.

THIS IS
GONNA BE
THE HARDEST
THING EVER.
SNRF

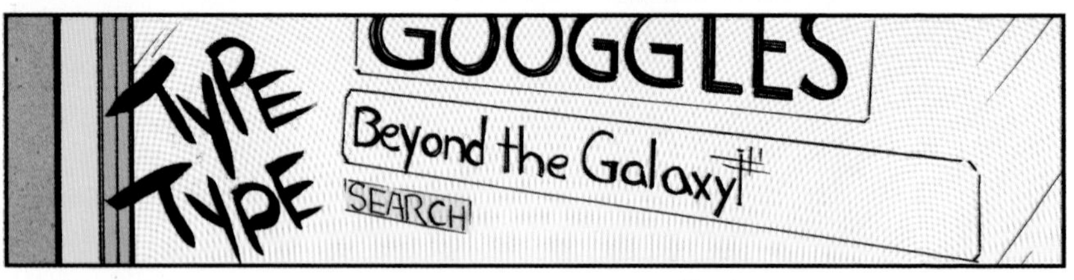
GOOGGLES
TYPE TYPE
Beyond the Galaxy
SEARCH

GOOOOG
SEARCH RESULTS
IMAGES
BEYOND THE GALAXY

WHATCHA DOING?
AHHH!

ELOUISE! DO YOU MIND? I'M USING THE COMPUTER!
WHY ARE YOU BEING ALL SNEAKY ABOUT IT?
DOGGO

I'M JUST LOOKING SOMETHING UP. IT'S NONE OF YOUR BUSINESS.
BEYOND THE GALAXY? IS THAT THE OLD SCI-FI SHOW?

...YES.
I REMEMBER THAT SHOW. THE CHEESY ALIEN MAKEUP, THOSE SETS THAT LOOKED LIKE THEY WERE MADE OUT OF FOAM...

I ALSO REMEMBER YOU DRESSING UP AS ONE OF THE CHARACTERS FOR HALLOWEEN. WHO WAS THE BLUE ALIEN LADY?
LIEUTENANT NEKO.

RIIIGHT. WOW, YOU WERE SUPER INTO IT FOR, LIKE, A YEAR. YOU'D GO TO GRAMMA'S HOUSE ALL THE TIME TO WATCH RERUNS.
WE DIDN'T HAVE CABLE. I COULDN'T WATCH IT HERE.

ALSO, THAT WAS THE YEAR MOM AND DAD BROKE UP, SO IT REALLY SUCKED BEING AT HOME.

OH... RIGHT.

BEYOND THE GALAXY

I LOVED CAPTAIN FINN. EVERY WEEK HE'D SAVE A PLANET, STOP A TIME-TRAVELING CRIMINAL... THAT KINDA THING.
AND HE NEVER YELLED AT HIS CREW.

MOM AND DAD YELLED SO MUCH WHEN THEY BROKE UP.

I GUESS I DIDN'T WATCH IT AS MUCH AFTER THAT YEAR.
WHY NOT?

I DUNNO. TAYLOR THOUGHT IT WAS A STUPID SHOW, AND I DIDN'T KNOW ANY OTHER GIRLS WHO WERE INTO IT.
TAYLOR'S WRONG. IT'S NOT STUPID.

EVEN THOUGH IT HAS CHEESY ALIEN MAKEUP AND FAKE FOAM SETS?
THAT'S PART OF THE CHARM: IT SHOWS THE WORK THAT WENT INTO THE SHOW. A SET DESIGNER SPENT HOURS CARVING THOSE FOAM ROCKS.

AND I BET THERE ARE LOTS OF GIRLS WHO LIKE *BEYOND THE GALAXY.*
WELL, I DON'T KNOW ANY.
EL DOGGO

WAIT. MAYBE I DO.
EL DOGGO

SATURDAY
HOW WAS YOUR FIRST RIDING CLASS, AMI?
SCARY.
SCARY? WHAT WAS SO SCARY?
HORSES ARE BIG AND SCARY BUT I LOVE THEM.

HORSES CAN
BE SCARY, I AGREE.
BUT OLAF IS A PONY,
AND PONIES AREN'T
SCARY, ARE THEY?
NO.
I LOVE
OLAF.

YOU'RE
THE BEST
PONY, OLAF.

HE'S A
GOOD BOY.
NOW LET'S GET
HIM UNTACKED
AND PUT
TO BED.

YOU'RE REALLY GOOD WITH HER. SHE WASN'T THAT RESPONSIVE WHEN I RODE HER.

ARE YOU SHUNNING ME TOO?

NO.

DO YOU LIKE
BEYOND THE GALAXY?

YES.
WHO TOLD YOU I DID?

THAT BOY WHO RIDES HERE. I DON'T KNOW HIS NAME, BUT HE'S THE ONLY BOY.
SAM.
YEAH, SAM.

I CAN'T TALK TO YOU UNLESS NORRIE IS OKAY WITH YOU.

YEAH, I KINDA MESSED THAT UP. YOU GUYS ARE CLOSE?

SHE'S MY BEST FRIEND.

I LIKE HORSES BECAUSE THEY DON'T CARE IF I TALK. AND NORRIE'S KIND OF LIKE THAT TOO.
STANLEY PARK

WHEN I FIRST MET NORRIE, SHE SAID YOU GUYS GET ALONG SO WELL BECAUSE SHE TALKS ENOUGH FOR TWO PEOPLE.

I NEVER HAVE TO WORRY ABOUT WEIRD SILENCES WHEN I TALK TO NORRIE. SHE MAKES IT EASY TO HAVE A CONVERSATION.

I USED TO HAVE SOMEONE LIKE THAT.

WHEN I FIRST CAME HERE, I DIDN'T WANT TO BE FRIENDS WITH ANY MORE HORSE GIRLS...

...BUT I THOUGHT, MAYBE IF YOU LIKED *BEYOND THE GALAXY*...
I DO.

THIS IS GONNA BE THE HARDEST THING EVER.

OLAF!

OLAF, GOSH DARN IT—

OLAF, NOOOO!

WHY ARE PONIES SO *EVIL??*
hff!
hff!

OLAF,
COME BACK!

I TOLD THAT GIRL YOU WERE A **NICE** PONY!

I HATE YOU.
I HATE YOU.
I HATE YOU.

HFF
HFF
HFF
MUNCH
MUNCH

NEED SOME HELP?

NOT FROM *YOU* I DON'T!
SHUN!

MUNCH
MUNCH

PONIES ARE THE WORST. THEY LOOK SWEET, BUT THEY'RE ACTUALLY PURE EVIL.

A GIRL RODE HIM THIS MORNING, HER FIRST RIDE EVER, AND HE WAS AN ABSOLUTE ANGEL.

THE MINUTE THE GIRL LEAVES, OLAF SLIPS HIS HALTER AND MAKES FOR THE HILLS.
WHAT A JERK.

YEAH, YOU HEARD ME! YOU'RE A JERK, OLAF!

PONIES HAVE NO SHAME.

I BROUGHT CARROTS.

OKAY. YOU GO RIGHT, I'LL GO LEFT. WHOEVER GETS CLOSEST, GRAB HIM.
MUNCH MUNCH

OLAF, I'VE GOT A TREAT FOR YOU.

MUNCH
MUNCH

GOOD BOY. YOU WANT A CARROT, DON'T YOU?

SURE YOU DO.

WHAT A GOOD BOY YOU ARE.

LET'S JUST SLIP THIS ON...
MUNCH
CRUNCH

FLING!

OOF!
WHAMM

SPLAT

NEEIIIIIGH

OH NOOOO!

OF COURSE I LAND IN THE ONLY MUD PUDDLE. HILARIOUS.
NO, IT'S NOT THAT.

WATCHING YOU PUT THE HALTER ON OLAF, IT WAS LIKE YOU HAD THESE AMAZING HORSE-CONTROLLING SUPERPOWERS. I'D BEEN CHASING HIM FOR HALF AN HOUR AND YOU JUST WALK UP AND PUT A HALTER ON HIM.

AND THEN, BAM! RIGHT IN THE MUD.
YEAH, NO SUPERPOWERS. PONIES MESS WITH ME AS MUCH AS THEY MESS WITH ANYONE ELSE.

WSST

WHY ARE YOU HERE, ANYWAY?
I WANTED TO SAY I'M SORRY FOR HOW I TREATED YOU WHEN WE MET.

YOU WERE BEING NICE. YOU WELCOMED ME TO EDGEWOOD. AND I WAS A JERK.

NO, NOT ***THAT.*** WHY ARE YOU HERE AT ***EDGEWOOD?***

IT'S KIND OF A LONG STORY.
I GOT TIME. JUST HANGING OUT IN A FIELD, CHASING A PONY WHO DOESN'T WANT TO BE CAUGHT.

WAVERLY STABLES IS THE PLACE YOU ***WANT*** TO RIDE AT, NOT EDGEWOOD. THEY HOST AMAZING SHOWS. THEY HAVE COOL RIDING CLINICS WITH FAMOUS INSTRUCTORS.
THEIR BARN FLOOR IS SO CLEAN YOU COULD EAT OFF IT.

IF YOU WANT TO BECOME A REALLY ***GOOD*** RIDER, YOU RIDE ***THERE,*** NOT HERE.
MUNCH
MUNCH
THAT WAS PART OF WHY I LEFT, ACTUALLY.

ALL I WANTED TO DO WAS ***RIDE.*** I DIDN'T WANT TO COMPETE. I DIDN'T WANT— I COULDN'T ***AFFORD*** THE RIDING CLINICS.

THERE'S PRESSURE AT WAVERLY TO BE A CERTAIN KIND OF RIDER. BUT THAT ISN'T THE WHOLE STORY OF WHY I LEFT.
SO, WHY DID YOU?

AT THE BEGINNING OF THE SUMMER, MY BEST FRIEND, TAYLOR, GOT HER VERY OWN HORSE.
FOR REAL?? OH MAN, *LUCKY.*

AND SHE DIDN'T WANT ME TO RIDE HIM.

WHAT?

THREE MONTHS AGO
WHAT?

I NEED TO DO WHAT'S BEST FOR KING.

WE'RE DOING REALLY INTENSIVE TRAINING FOR THE TRILLIUM CIRCUIT, AND I DON'T THINK IT'S A GOOD IDEA FOR SOMEONE WHO'S NOT UP TO A CERTAIN LEVEL TO RIDE HIM.
NOT...UP TO ***A CERTAIN LEVEL??*** WHAT DOES ***THAT*** MEAN??

YOU DON'T SEEM TO CARE ABOUT RIDING AS MUCH AS I DO—
THAT'S *CRAZY!* I RIDE JUST AS MUCH AS YOU DO! AND THEN I MUCK OUT STALLS TO PAY FOR EXTRA LESSONS.

GROUP LESSONS AREN'T THE SAME AS ONE-ON-ONE INSTRUCTION WITH MR. ROSEN.
I CAN'T ***AFFORD*** PRIVATE LESSONS! AND I'M A ***GOOD*** RIDER!

I'M JUST AS GOOD AS YOU AND YOU KNOW IT.

THEN MAYBE YOU'RE NOT AS ***DEDICATED*** AS I AM. YOU USED TO BE, BUT NOT ANYMORE.

YOU FOUND A WAY TO PAY FOR PRIVATE LESSONS LAST SUMMER.
I WORKED AT WAVERLY *EVERY DAY* TO PAY FOR THOSE! MAYBE I DON'T *WANT* TO DO THAT THIS SUMMER. MAYBE I WANT A *BREAK*.

IT FEELS LIKE—LIKE YOU DON'T CARE ABOUT HORSES ANYMORE.

HOW CAN YOU *SAY* THAT? I *LOVE* HORSES. I JUST WANT TIME FOR OTHER THINGS AS WELL.

I GOTTA GO.

MUNCH
MUNCH

IT'S STUPID.
WOW, IT IS SO NOT STUPID!

IF SOMEDAY MY PARENTS MAGICALLY WIN THE LOTTERY AND BUY ME MY VERY OWN HORSE, OF COURSE I'LL LET HAZEL RIDE IT! SHE'S MY BEST FRIEND.

THAT'S THE POINT OF HAVING STABLE FRIENDS! YOU SHARE YOUR LOVE OF HORSES WITH THEM.

YEAH.

WHAT IF HAZEL STOPPED LOVING HORSES THE SAME WAY YOU DID?

I'D BE SAD IF SHE STOPPED RIDING, BUT I WOULDN'T STOP BEING HER FRIEND.

I GUESS WE'D, LIKE, BOND OVER *BEYOND THE GALAXY* OR WHATEVER. WE'D FIND SOMETHING ELSE TO SHARE.
MUNCH
MUNCH

AND I'D STILL LET HER RIDE MY HORSE, IF SHE EVER WANTED TO.

UM...IF I COULD GO BACK IN TIME AND TELL MYSELF NOT TO BE A JERK TO YOU WHEN I FIRST CAME TO EDGEWOOD, I *REALLY* WOULD.

YEAH, TOO BAD THE TIME PORTAL FROM THE "RETURN TO TOMORROW" EPISODE OF *BEYOND THE GALAXY* DOESN'T EXIST IN REAL LIFE.

BUT IF YOU WANT TO MAKE IT UP TO ME, THERE *IS* SOMETHING YOU CAN DO.
WHAT IS IT?

I WANT TO HELP TRAIN THAT NEW LESSON HORSE.
WINTER?

YEAH. WILL YOU TALK TO MS. A ABOUT IT?
I CAN TOTALLY DO THAT.
AWESOME.

HUH, LOOK WHO'S DECIDED HE'S READY TO GO BACK TO THE BARN.

I SWEAR, OLAF, YOU'RE EVIL ON FOUR LEGS. DON'T TRY TO DENY IT.

CAPTAIN, WE'RE OUT OF TIME! THE INTRA-DIMENSIONAL RIFT BOMB WILL GO OFF IN SEVEN SECONDS!
THEN WE'LL *MAKE* MORE TIME!
LIEUTENANT NEKO!
DEET
HERE, CAPTAIN!
WE HAVE A LOCK ON YOU AND FIRST OFFICER JOSAFINA—
NO, DON'T USE THE CONVEYOR, I NEED *MORE TIME!*
THE BOMB, SHE HAS THE BOMB—

TOO LATE, CAPTAIN FINN.

WAAAGGGH.

AND THAT'S THE LAST EPISODE OF *BEYOND THE GALAXY* SEASON THREE.
TO BE CONTINUED
HOW COULD THEY END IT LIKE THAT???

YOU REALLY HADN'T SEEN THE FINAL EPISODE OF SEASON THREE?
NO! I MEAN, IT WAS A ***CHOICE***. PROBABLY THE RIGHT CHOICE. I DON'T THINK I COULD'VE HANDLED WATCHING THAT BACK WHEN IT FIRST AIRED.

BTG'S CREATORS SUPPOSEDLY HAD A WHOLE SEVEN-SEASON ARC PLANNED OUT, BUT EVERYTHING GOT MESSED UP WHEN THE NETWORK CANCELED THE SHOW.

SO THEY ENDED SEASON THREE ON A CLIFF-HANGER JUST TO STICK IT TO THE NETWORK.
HAHA, OH MAN, THAT'S SO MEAN.

AND NOW, ***FINALLY,*** THE STORY WILL BE CONCLUDED, YEARS AFTER ITS UNJUST CANCELATION! ALL THE SAME ACTORS ARE COMING BACK, MOST OF THE SAME WRITERS—IT'S GONNA BE AMAZING.
WILL THEY EXPLAIN WHY THE ACTORS ARE OLDER? IT'LL BE WEIRD IF SEASON FOUR PICKS UP RIGHT AFTER SEASON THREE AND EVERYONE'S, LIKE, TWENTY YEARS OLDER FOR NO REASON.

STOP ***NITPICKING!*** I COULDN'T SLEEP FOR ***WEEKS*** AFTER WATCHING SEASON THREE. WE WERE ***ROBBED*** OF AN ENDING AND NOW WE ***FINALLY*** GET ONE.
SAM, I LIKE THE SHOW TOO. GEEZ, CALM DOWN.

I GET IT.
YOU DO?

THE FIRST EPISODE OF THAT STORY ENDS WITH A CLIFF-HANGER—FIRST OFFICER JOSAFINA TRAPPED ON EARTH DURING THE 1600S, THE TIME PORTAL DESTROYED.

I SAW THE FIRST PART OF "RETURN TO TOMORROW" AT THE END OF MY SUMMER BREAK, BUT I DIDN'T GET TO SEE THE CONCLUSION UNTIL CHRISTMAS.

FOR THOSE MONTHS ALL I COULD THINK ABOUT WAS HOW WOULD FIRST OFFICER JOSAFINA GET BACK TO THE SHIP? WOULD SHE DAMAGE THE PAST AND DESTROY CAPTAIN FINN, LIKE THE SPACE ORACLE HAD PREDICTED?
RIP CAPTAIN FINN
I'D PLAY THE STORY OVER AND OVER IN MY MIND, TRYING TO FIGURE OUT WHAT WOULD HAPPEN, HOW EVERYTHING WOULD WORK OUT.
IT WAS SUCH A RELIEF TO FINALLY WATCH THE CONCLUSION. IT WAS MUCH LESS COMPLICATED THAN WHAT I WAS BUILDING UP IN MY HEAD, BUT FINALLY I COULD STOP THINKING ABOUT IT.

WHY DIDN'T YOU JUST LOOK UP THE EPISODE SUMMARY ON WIKIPEDIA?

GASP
GASP

IGNORE HER. A TRUE FAN UNDERSTANDS.

I'M NOT SURE I ACTUALLY WANT TO SEE WHAT HAPPENS IN SEASON FOUR.
REALLY?

THE STORY'S NEVER GOING TO BE AS GOOD AS THE ONE I IMAGINE. WHY NOT KEEP IT A MYSTERY? THEN I WON'T BE DISAPPOINTED.
NAH, EVEN IF I'M DISAPPOINTED, I STILL GOTTA KNOW THE END.

I GOTTA KNOW.

NORRIE?

IT'S A SCHOOL NIGHT. MOM AND DAD SAID YOUR FRIENDS NEED TO GO HOME BEFORE IT GETS TOO LATE.
UGH, FINE!

TWO WEEKS! ONLY FOURTEEN MORE DAYS AND SEASON FOUR OF *BTG* IS ***HERE!***
WE STILL HAVEN'T DECIDED WHAT WE'RE GOING TO DO TO CELEBRATE.

I THOUGHT WE WERE DRESSING UP.
YEAH, BUT THEN WHAT? JUST SIT AROUND IN OUR *BTG* COSPLAY? SHOULDN'T WE GO SOMEWHERE?

HMM. I DUNNO.
WE'LL FIGURE SOMETHING OUT. WE'VE GOT TIME.

G'NIGHT, YOU NERRRDS!
DON'T FORGET TO STUDY, NORRIE.

YEAH, YEAH.
SLAMM

HEY, VICTORIA...

I HAVE AN EXTRA *BTG* PATCH, IF YOU WANT IT.
BTG

I *DO* WANT IT! THANK YOU.

I, UH, ALSO HAVE AN EXTRA POSTCARD, IF YOU WANT THAT AS WELL.
OH, YES PLEASE!

WELCOME TO THE FANDOM.

I'M HOME.
'SUP. THERE'S CURRY IN THE FRIDGE IF YOU'RE HUNGRY. MOM'S WORKING LATE.

THANKS. I'LL EAT IN A BIT.

THMP
THMP

TOSS

NEKO
BTG

STICK!

NEKO

NORRIE'S HELPING YOU TRAIN WINTER?
YEAH, I COULDN'T DO IT ALL ON MY OWN.

A GOOD SCHOOLING HORSE NEEDS TO BE USED TO DIFFERENT RIDERS, SO THIS IS GREAT FOR HIM.

HELLO, ALL, GATHER ROUND FOR A MINUTE.

YOU TOO, NORRIE.

I JUST GOT OFF THE PHONE WITH RACHEL PAGE, WHO OWNS WAVERLY STABLES. THIS YEAR THEY'VE DECIDED TO INVITE ALL THE LOCAL BARNS TO JOIN THEIR ANNUAL SCHOOLING SHOW.

WAVERLY STABLES??
YES, YOU KNOW, THE STABLE EAST OF US, CLOSE TO WAVERLY LAKE?

OUR *NEMESIS!*

DON'T BE SILLY, NORRIE. THEY'RE A LOVELY BUNCH OF PEOPLE. I'VE KNOWN RACHEL FOR YEARS.

...OUR NEMESIS.

NORRIE AND VICTORIA, YOU'VE BOTH DONE A WONDERFUL JOB WORKING WITH WINTER. I THINK IT'D BE GOOD EXPERIENCE FOR HIM IF HE WENT TO A SCHOOLING SHOW.
HAZEL AND SAM, YOU'RE ALSO WELCOME TO ATTEND WITH YOUR FAVORITE SCHOOLING HORSE. I'LL HANDLE THE TRANSPORTATION.

WHAT DO YOU THINK? WANT TO GO?

YES!
...NO.

I'LL LEAVE YOU TO FIGURE IT OUT. LET ME KNOW THIS THURSDAY, ALL RIGHT?

HAZEL, YOU REALLY DON'T WANT TO GO TO THE SHOW?
NO.

WHY NOT? THIS IS OUR CHANCE TO PROVE EDGEWOOD'S RIDERS ARE JUST AS GOOD AS WAVERLY'S.

UGH.

DO YOU MIND WALKING HIM?
SURE.

SO WHY DON'T *YOU* WANT TO GO TO THE SHOW?
IF IT WERE ANYWHERE ELSE, I'D PROBABLY GO. BUT I'M NOT GOING BACK TO WAVERLY.

OH.
IT'S NOT A BIG DEAL. NORRIE CAN RIDE WINTER IN THE SHOW. HE'LL BE FINE WITH HER.

BUT HE'S BEEN WORKING WITH YOU FOR LONGER. ISN'T IT BETTER FOR THE HORSE IF HE'S RIDDEN BY THE RIDER HE'S USED TO?

I FEEL GUILTY ABOUT IT ALREADY, SAM. I JUST...I CAN'T GO BACK THERE.

OKAY THEN.

HAZEL!

THNK

HEY, WHAT'S UP?
YOU *KNOW* WHY I DON'T WANT TO COMPETE.

SO YOU FROZE UP BEFORE A SHOW ONE TIME. IT WAS YEARS AGO.
IT FEELS LIKE *YESTERDAY.*

I PRACTICED SO MUCH. I WANTED IT TO HAPPEN.

I SAW IT IN MY HEAD. THE PERFECT RIDE.

I COULDN'T EVEN MAKE MYSELF GO IN THE RING.

IT HURT SO MUCH.

IT'S JUST A SCHOOLING SHOW. IF YOU DON'T WANT TO GO, NO ONE'S GONNA CARE.

BUT *I* CARE.

WHAT IF... YOU CAME TO THE SHOW TO SUPPORT ME?

YOU WOULDN'T HAVE TO COMPETE. YOU COULD JUST BE AT THE SHOW AS MY FRIEND.

AND IF YOU FELT LIKE RIDING AT SOME POINT, YOU COULD. IF YOU DIDN'T, YOU WOULDN'T HAVE TO.

BUT THERE ARE SHOW ENTRY FEES AND TRANSPORTATION COSTS FOR THE HORSES...
I'LL WORK SOMETHING OUT WITH MS. A.

WHAT IF I CAN'T GO INTO THE RING AGAIN?

THEN YOU'RE JUST AT THE SHOW TO SUPPORT ME.

IT'LL BE A FUN DAY! YOU CAN SEE ME GET MY BUTT KICKED BY THOSE PERFECT WAVERLY STABLES RIDERS.

NAH.
AW, REALLY?

NAH, YOU'RE GONNA BEAT THOSE WAVERLY RIDERS. AND I'LL BE THERE TO SEE IT.

WE'RE GONNA END UP LITERALLY ***COVERED*** IN RIBBONS.

STICK!
Lt NEKO
BEYOND THE GALAXY
USS VIGILANCE
UNITED

Lt NEKO
BEYOND THE GALAXY

VIC!
YOUR FRIENDS ARE HERE!

THE ONLY REASON I GOT TO GO OUT ON A SCHOOL NIGHT IS BECAUSE I TOLD MY PARENTS WE WERE ALL STUDYING TOGETHER.

LITTLE DO THEY KNOW! MUAHAHA!
BUT YOU DID STUDY FOR THAT TEST WE HAVE TOMORROW, RIGHT?

I STUDIED! I GOT ALL THE GOOD LOUIS RIEL FACTS LOCKED INSIDE MY BRAIN.
OKAY, JUST CHECKING.

HERE'S WHAT I'VE BEEN WORKING ON.

TAA DAAA

WOW, THAT LOOKS GREAT!

DID YOU MAKE IT ALL YOURSELF?
KINDA. I FOUND THE JUMPSUIT AT A THRIFT STORE. I DID ALL THE COLOR SECTIONS MYSELF, AND SAM TOLD ME WHERE I COULD BUY THE PATCHES.

IT'S NOT PERFECT, BUT I'M REALLY HAPPY WITH IT.
IT'S *AWESOME.*

I SUDDENLY REGRET TRYING TO MAKE A UNIFORM FROM SCRATCH. USING A SECONDHAND JUMPSUIT WOULD'VE BEEN MUCH EASIER.
YOU'VE STILL GOT TWO WEEKS UNTIL THE PREMIERE.

SO ARE WE JUST GOING TO WATCH THE NEW SEASON IN OUR COSTUMES? SEEMS LIKE A LOT OF WORK TO JUST STAY IN NORRIE'S BASEMENT.

WE COULD WEAR THEM TO SCHOOL?

I ALREADY GET SO MUCH CRAP FROM THEM BECAUSE I RIDE HORSES.

THEY'RE ALWAYS, LIKE, OH, THAT'S NOT A *REAL* SPORT! THE *HORSE* DOES ALL THE WORK.

AND THEN THEY ASK ME WHY I'M HANGING OUT WITH GIRLS IF I DON'T WANT TO DATE THEM.
NO OFFENSE, BUT YOUR BROTHERS KINDA SUCK, SAM.

UGH, I DON'T WANT TO THINK ABOUT THEM. LET'S GET THESE UNIFORMS FINISHED.

WE STILL NEED TO DECIDE WHAT WE'RE ACTUALLY GOING TO DO WITH THEM.

WE NEED *SOMEWHERE* TO WEAR THEM. SOMEWHERE WE CAN TAKE PICTURES, SHOW OFF OUR COOL THREADS.

SOMEWHERE THAT ISN'T SCHOOL, AND DOESN'T MEAN WE HAVE TO BUILD A REPLICA OF THE *STARCRAFT VIGILANCE*'S BRIDGE IN MY PARENTS' BASEMENT.
TUG

ACTUALLY... I THINK I HAVE AN IDEA.

TWO DAYS LATER...

HISTORY TEST
D-

NO NO NO
NOOOOO.

NORRIE! YOU TOLD ME YOU STUDIED!
I DID! I HAD ALL THE LOUIS RIEL FACTS LOCKED IN MY BRAIN!

JUST TURNED OUT THEY WERE THE WRONG FACTS.

WHAT WILL YOUR PARENTS DO?
THEY'LL GROUND ME UNTIL I'M THIRTY, FOR STARTERS.

NORRIE, BE SERIOUS.
I AM BEING SERIOUS! YOU'RE LOOKING AT SOMEONE WHO ISN'T LEAVING THE HOUSE FOR THE NEXT SEVENTEEN YEARS!

OKAY, REALISTICALLY THEY'LL PROBABLY GROUND ME FOR A MONTH. NO RIDING, NO GOING OUT, JUST STUDYING UNTIL MY GRADES COME BACK UP.
BUT... THE WAVERLY SCHOOLING SHOW IS NEXT WEEK.

YEAH, THERE'S NO WAY THEY'RE GONNA LET ME GO TO THAT.
AND THE *BTG* SEASON FOUR PREMIERE IS THE WEEK AFTER THAT.

MY LIFE IS RUINED.
ASK TAHIR FOR HELP.

TAHIR? HE'S NOT GONNA HELP ME. MISTER PERFECT STRAIGHT A'S FOREVER, BLEH.

HE WILL. HE'S ALWAYS HELPED YOU. HE DRIVES US TO EDGEWOOD ALL THE TIME. HE MAKES SURE YOU'RE DOING YOUR HOMEWORK EVEN THOUGH YOU'RE KIND OF A JERK TO HIM.
I AM NOT!

OKAY, MAYBE I AM A LITTLE.

ASK HIM FOR HELP. IT'S WORTH A TRY.

TAHIR'S
ROOM

SIIIGHH

TAHIR?
TAHIR'S
ROOM
YEAH?

UM, MIND IF I TALK TO YOU ABOUT SOMETHING?
SURE.

I BOMBED A TEST AND MOM AND DAD ARE GOING TO GROUND ME FOREVER AND THERE'S A HORSE SHOW COMING UP THAT'S ***REALLY IMPORTANT!*** I ***HAVE*** TO BE THERE!

AND THE NEW *BEYOND THE GALAXY* SHOW IS STARTING IN ***TWO WEEKS*** AND ALL MY FRIENDS MADE COSTUMES AND I MADE A COSTUME AND I DON'T KNOOOW WHAT TO DOOOOO!

WHOA, HANG ON!
IT'S NOT FAIR I HAVE TO BE AS PERFECT AS YOU ARE! IT'S NOT FAAAIR!

SNF
SNF

SHRUG
OH MAN, NORRIE, I AM ***NOT*** PERFECT.

YOU ARE! YOU GET AMAZING GRADES. DAD IS ALWAYS BRAGGING ABOUT HOW ***SMART*** YOU ARE.
SNFF
SNFF
SNF

BUT I STUDY ALL THE TIME! I DON'T HAVE—I MEAN, NOT THE WAY ***YOU*** HAVE—
SNF

I HAVE WHAT?

I THINK IT'S REALLY COOL HOW MANY FRIENDS YOU HAVE. I SPEND SO MUCH TIME GRINDING AWAY ON SCHOOLWORK, I'VE NEVER BEEN GOOD AT MAKING FRIENDS.
I'VE ONLY MADE TWO FRIENDS IN HIGH SCHOOL, AND THEY'RE BOTH GUYS FROM THE ROBOTICS CLUB WHO I DON'T EVEN LIKE.

OH... I DIDN'T KNOW THAT.

IT'S OKAY. GRADUATION IS IN ONE MORE YEAR AND I'M GONNA EASE OFF AFTER THAT. MAKE SOME REAL FRIENDS AT COLLEGE.

YEAH, YOU SHOULD. FRIENDS ARE GREAT.
SO I'VE HEARD.

LET'S TALK TO MOM AND DAD TOGETHER, OKAY?
OKAY. SNIFF.

I TOLD YOU TAHIR WOULD HELP.
AUDITIONS
WELL, I AM STILL GROUNDED.

BUT AT LEAST YOU GET TO SEE THE BTG PREMIERE. WINTER MISSING A SCHOOLING SHOW ISN'T THAT BIG A DEAL.
OH NO, WINTER'S NOT MISSING THE SHOW.

BUT YOU WON'T BE THERE TO RIDE HIM—
I WON'T BE, BUT YOU WILL. YOU CAN TAKE HIM TO THE SHOW.

NO, I CAN'T.
YOU CAN! YOU'RE THE ONE WHO'S WORKED WITH HIM THE MOST THESE PAST TWO MONTHS.

YOU'RE THE ONE WHO SHOULD BE RIDING HIM ANYWAY, NOT ME.

IT'S NOT HAPPENING. I'M SORRY.

DRAMA! IT'S THE WORST.

READ

WHAT WOULD HAPPEN IF YOU WENT TO WAVERLY STABLES?
I'D SEE MY EX-BEST FRIEND.

AND?
AND...AND I DON'T *WANT* TO SEE HER!

ARE YOU GOING TO TELL ME TO BE TOUGH AND FACE MY FEARS?
YIKES, THAT SOUNDS TERRIBLE. WHY WOULD I SAY THAT?

I DUNNO, SEEMS LIKE SOMETHING BOYS SAY TO THEIR FRIENDS.
DOES IT SEEM LIKE SOMETHING I'D SAY TO *MY* FRIENDS?

NO, OF COURSE NOT.

READ

WHAT HAPPENS IF YOU ***DON'T*** GO TO THE WAVERLY SCHOOLING SHOW?
NOTHING, I GUESS. I KEEP RIDING AT EDGEWOOD. I CONTINUE TRAINING WINTER.

WOULD IT BE GOOD FOR WINTER IF YOU WENT TO THE SHOW?
I THINK SO. IT'D GIVE HIM A CHANCE TO COMPETE AND GET USED TO CROWDS.

IT MIGHT BOOST HIS CONFIDENCE IF HE HAD A GOOD DAY.

AND YOU WANT THAT FOR HIM, RIGHT?

YEAH, HE'S A REALLY GREAT HORSE; HE JUST NEEDS TO BUILD UP HIS COURAGE. TO SEE THAT THE WORLD OUTSIDE HIS STALL ISN'T SCARY AND OUT TO GET HIM.

AND...
MAYBE I
NEED THAT
AS WELL.

I KEEP BUILDING WAVERLY UP IN MY MIND. LIKE, WHAT HAPPENED THERE WITH TAYLOR IS SOMETHING I PRETEND I'M ***FINE*** WITH. IF I JUST IGNORE IT, ACT LIKE IT DIDN'T HAPPEN, I'LL BE ***FINE.***

AND IF YOU KEEP PRETENDING YOU'RE FINE, YOU'LL STOP FEELING BAD ABOUT IT, RIGHT? BUT THAT'S NOT HOW IT WORKS, IS IT?

NOPE. NOT HOW IT WORKS AT ALL.

SIIIGH.

RETU
I DON'T WANT TO DO THIS.
YOU DON'T HAVE TO.

NO, I DO. FOR WINTER.

YEAH. FOR WINTER.

WE'VE GOT ONE MORE WEEK TO PREPARE FOR THE SHOW. LET'S MAKE IT HAPPEN.

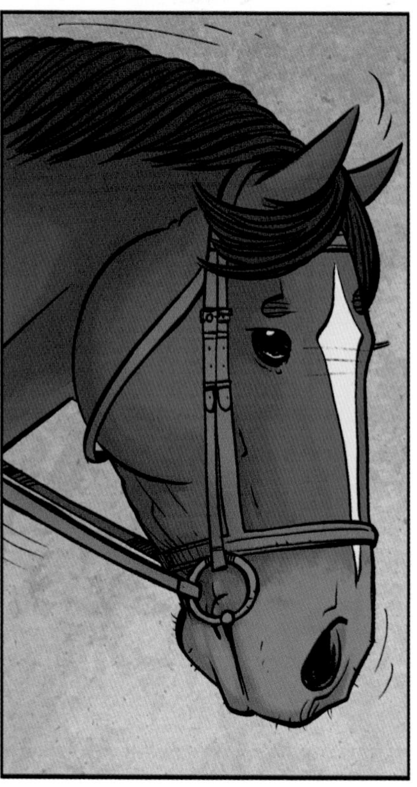

KATHNK
KATHNK

LOOKING GOOD!
HE'S SO GREAT. I LOVE WORKING WITH HIM.

MS. A SAID YOU'LL BE SHOWING HIM TOMORROW.
YEAH, IF YOU THINK WE'RE READY.

WE'LL SEE HOW HE HANDLES THINGS, BUT YOU BOTH LOOK GOOD TODAY.

I BELIEVE IN YOU, WINTER.
SNORT

WOW, FANCY!
OH, RIGHT, YOU'VE NEVER BEEN HERE BEFORE.

HOW ARE YOU DOING?
I'M OKAY, ACTUALLY.

I'M HERE FOR WINTER.

WHAT A
GOOD BOY.

YOU'RE DOING
SO WELL.

HE SEEMS PRETTY CHILL.
YEAH, HE HANDLED THE TRAILER RIDE OVER REALLY WELL.

I'M SO PROUD OF YOU. WHAT A GOOD FELLA.
SMK

HOW'S QUINN DOING?
SHE'S FINE.

SHE'S CALMER THAN ME, TO BE HONEST.

I'M REALLY SORRY NORRIE COULDN'T COME.
ME TOO. I FEEL SO MUCH BRAVER WHEN SHE'S WITH ME.

SHE'S NOT AFRAID OF TALKING TO PEOPLE SHE DOESN'T KNOW OR HAVING THEM THINK SHE'S WEIRD, AND I'M NOT EITHER WHEN I'M WITH HER.

LET'S SEND HER A PHOTO. EVERYONE SAY "EDGEWOOD!"
CLICK!
EDGEWOOD!

WISH YOU WERE HERE, NORRIE.
SEND

OHHHH NO.

YO, SAM!
WHOA.

WHO'RE THEY?
SAM'S BROTHERS. WHAT ARE THEY *DOING* HERE?

WHAT ARE YOU *DOING* HERE??

DAD DROPPED US OFF.
WE'RE HERE TO WATCH OUR BRO *RIDE!*
WHY??

HEY, DO WE NEED A REASON? WE WANTED TO CHECK OUT THIS EQUESTRIAN THING YOU'RE ALWAYS GOING ON ABOUT.
SHOW US HOW YOU TAME THESE WILD BEASTS!

DO THEY NOT KNOW HORSES ARE DOMESTICATED...?

GOOD LUCK, BRO! WE'LL BE WATCHING!

SAM?

I'M FINE. IT'S FINE. IT'S FINE! I'M FINE!

YOU LOOK GOOD.
YEAH, I OWE NORRIE BIG TIME FOR LOANING ME THE JACKET.

WHAT DOES A PERFECT RIDE FEEL LIKE?

IT'S... LIKE MUSIC.

WINNING A RIBBON DOESN'T MAKE A RIDE PERFECT. THE ONLY THING THAT MATTERS IS THE FEELING THAT HAPPENS WHEN YOU AND YOUR HORSE ARE PERFECTLY IN SYNC.

LIKE MUSIC.

NUMBER TWENTY-THREE.

YOU CAN DO IT!
GO HAZEL, GO!

Whewww

QUINN, LET'S GO.

23

GOOD GIRL,
QUINN.

OH NO.

SIGH

WHAT WAS THAT ABOUT?
I MISSED A JUMP ON THE COURSE, SO I GOT DISQUALIFIED.
23

BUT I HEARD IT! I HEARD THE MUSIC! IT WAS *PERFECT.*

THEN THAT'S ALL THAT MATTERS.

YOU CAN DO IT! I BELIEVE!
HAHA, I BELIEVE TOO.

27

HI.

HI...UM, HI, ARE YOU RIDING?
NO, I RODE KING AT A TRILLIUM SHOW LAST WEEK, SO I'M GIVING HIM A BREAK.

I MEAN, IT'S JUST A SCHOOLING SHOW. IT'S JUST FOR FUN, RIGHT?

YEAH. I GUESS? IT DOESN'T MATTER.

NUMBER TWENTY-SEVEN.

I—
I GOTTA GO.

GOOD LUCK, VICTORIA!

IT DOESN'T MATTER.
IT DOESN'T MATTER.
JUST FOCUS—

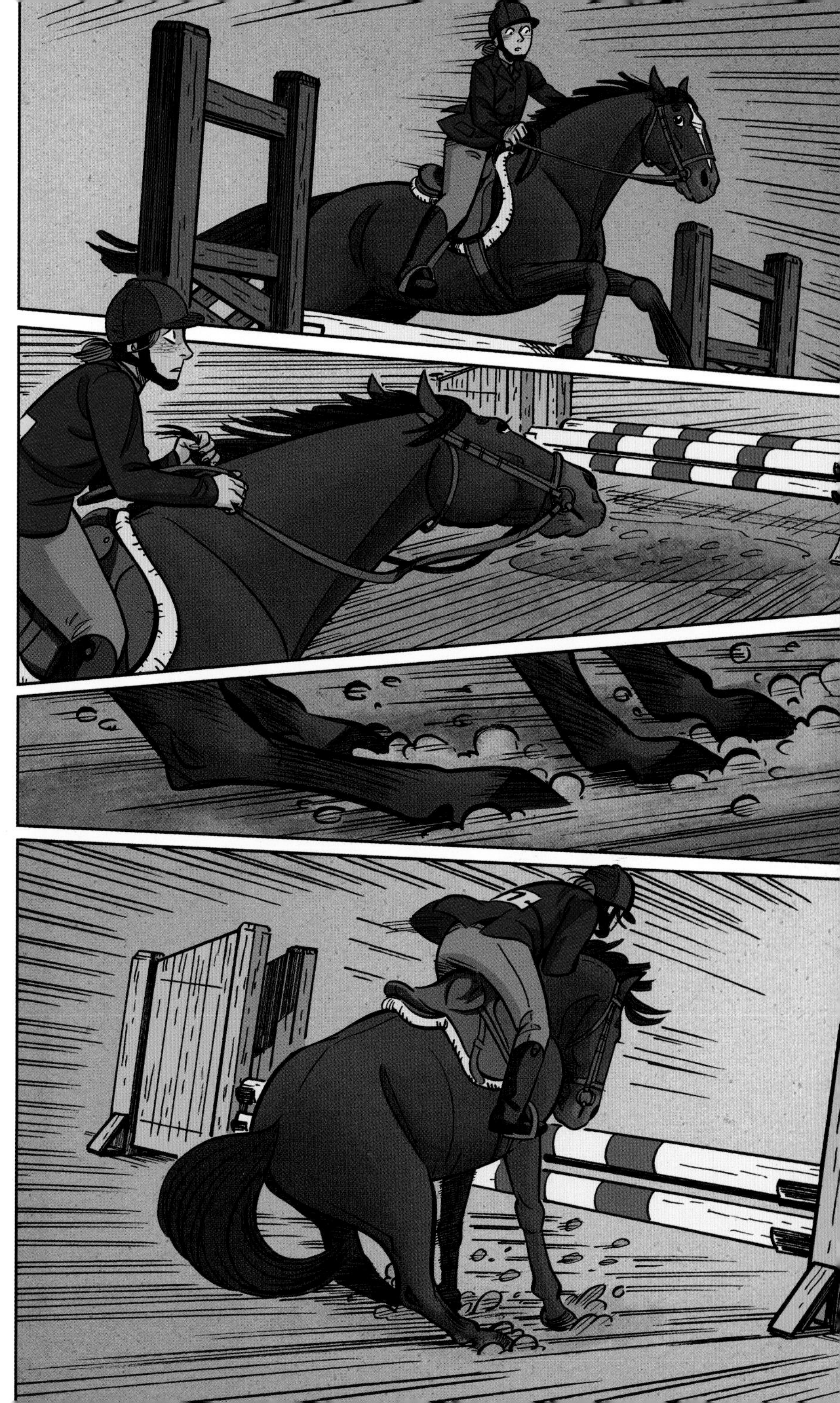

WHUDD

hahh

27

I'M SORRY.

SNORT

I WASN'T PAYING ATTENTION TO WHAT YOU NEEDED. I LET YOU DOWN.

I'M REALLY SORRY.

FWIIING
SNORT!

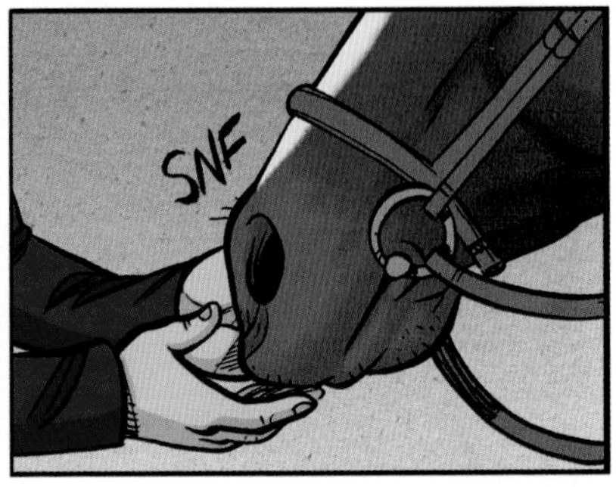
SNF

CAN WE TRY AGAIN?
WILL YOU TRUST ME?

SNRF

27

THANK YOU.

LET'S GO.

YOU DID SO GOOD, WINTER.

ARE YOU OKAY?
YEAH, THE GROUND WAS PRETTY SOFT.
27
I'M GOING TO WALK WINTER FOR A BIT THEN TAKE HIM BACK TO THE TRAILER.

HAHA, YOU'RE SUCH A GOOBER.
SNRF

THAT'S THE FIRST TIME I'VE SEEN YOU FALL OFF.

IT WAS PRETTY EMBARRASSING. MY SHOULDER'S GONNA BRUISE FOR SURE.

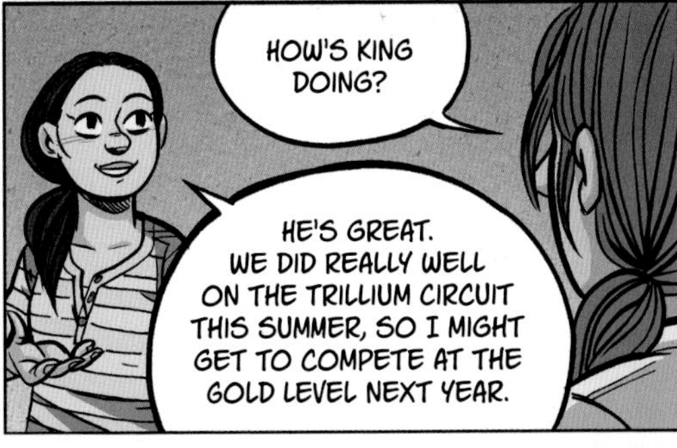
HOW'S KING DOING?
HE'S GREAT. WE DID REALLY WELL ON THE TRILLIUM CIRCUIT THIS SUMMER, SO I MIGHT GET TO COMPETE AT THE GOLD LEVEL NEXT YEAR.

THAT'S A REALLY BIG DEAL.

YEAH. WE'RE BOTH WORKING REALLY HARD.

I THOUGHT... I THOUGHT IF I SAID YOU COULDN'T RIDE KING, MAYBE YOU'D WANT TO WORK HARDER AT IMPROVING YOUR RIDING.

LIKE, IT WOULD BE A *CHALLENGE.*

YOU'D GO BACK TO THE WAY YOU USED TO BE, WHEN HORSES WERE EVERYTHING TO YOU.
SNRF

THE WAY *I* AM.

I STILL LOVE HORSES, TAYLOR.
LICK
LICK
I KNOW, BUT IT'S NOT THE SAME.

YOU'RE RIGHT, IT'S NOT. BUT IT ISN'T ***WRONG*** TO WANT TO DO OTHER THINGS.

I DON'T WANT TO WIN SHOW RIBBONS. I DON'T WANT TO TRAIN EVERY FREE MINUTE. I WANT TO RIDE AND HANG OUT AT THE BARN, THAT'S ALL.

YEAH, YOU TOLD ME.

HEY, DO YOU REMEMBER THAT SCI-FI SHOW, *BEYOND THE GALAXY?*

THAT CHEESY SPACE SHOW? THE ONE WITH THE TERRIBLE SPECIAL EFFECTS?
THAT'S THE ONE.

WHAT ABOUT IT?
THERE'S A NEW *BEYOND THE GALAXY* SHOW STARTING NEXT WEEK. I'M REALLY EXCITED ABOUT IT.

SERIOUSLY? ***THAT'S*** WHAT YOU'RE EXCITED ABOUT?

YEAH, I AM.

WELL, SEE YOU AROUND, I GUESS.
SEE YOU.

YOOOO, GUESS WHO WON THE TOP EQUESTRIAN PRIZE!
IT'S OUR BRO SAM!

HE LEFT THOSE OTHER RIDERS IN THE *DIRT!*
SHOWED THEM WHO WAS *BEST!* HE'S A LEGEND!

CONGRATS, SAM.
THANKS. ROCKET DID GREAT—I'M REALLY HAPPY WITH OUR RIDE.
YO, IT WAS *AMAZING!*

IT WAS *POWERFUL!*
SO *POWERFUL!*
THEY LOST THEIR MINDS WHEN ROCKET CLEARED THE LAST JUMP. IT WAS SO FUNNY.

MAYBE NOW THEY'LL STOP TEASING YOU ABOUT HOW RIDING ISN'T A REAL SPORT?
MAYBE. BUT THEY *ARE* STILL MY BROTHERS. TEASING COMES WITH THE TERRITORY.

SORRY THINGS DIDN'T WORK OUT FOR YOU.
ACTUALLY, I THINK I'M OKAY WITH HOW THE DAY WENT.

SNF
IS IT WEIRD THAT RIGHT NOW I FEEL THE MOST OKAY I'VE FELT IN A LONG TIME?

NAH, THAT'S NOT WEIRD AT ALL.

WHUMP!

THIS STABLE IS *BEAUTIFUL.*

YEAH, BUT I CAN'T WAIT TO GET BACK HOME TO EDGEWOOD.

TWO WEEKS LATER

RENAISSANCE FESTIVAL

GUYS, I'M HAVING SOME DOUBTS. I'LL STILL GET YOU THE EMPLOYEE DISCOUNT ENTRY, BUT AFTER THAT, I DUNNO—

THERE ISN'T ANYTHING ON THE WEBSITE THAT SAID WE ***COULDN'T*** DO THIS.

THIS FAIR IS REALLY CUTE! WE SHOULD COME BACK SOME TIME FOR REAL.
IF WE'RE NOT BANNED FOR LIFE.

EVERYONE READY?

THIS IS CAPTAIN FINN OF THE *STARCRAFT VIGILANCE.* WE'VE BEEN CONVEYED DOWN TO AN ALIEN PLANET IN SEARCH OF A MISSING CREWMEMBER, BUT ***SOMETHING*** HAS GONE ***HORRIBLY WRONG.***

CAPTAIN FINN, THIS ***PLANET,*** THESE ***PEOPLE!*** THIS IS ***NO*** UNDISCOVERED FRONTIER!
GOSH DARN IT, FIRST OFFICER JOSAFINA! ***WHAT*** ARE YOU TRYING TO TELL ME?

IS THIS PART OF THE FAIR?
IT DOESN'T SEEM VERY HISTORICALLY ACCURATE.

THIS PLANET IS AN *EXACT* REPLICA OF EARTH DURING THE TIME PERIOD KNOWN AS... THE *RENAISSANCE*.

I REALLY HOPE NO ONE FROM SCHOOL IS HERE.

A REPLICA OF EARTH? HOW CAN IT *BE?*
CAPTAIN, IF I MAY. WE MIGHT HAVE BEEN CAUGHT IN AN *INTRA-DIMENSIONAL TIME VORTEX*.

CURSE YOUR ULTRA LOGICAL ALIEN BRAIN, ENSIGN SI! HOW CAN YOU BE SO CALM?
BE STILL, LIEUTENANT NEKO. WE MUST KEEP OUR WITS ABOUT US IF WE'RE TO SURVIVE THIS.

OH, I GET IT. THIS IS THAT OLD TV SHOW *BEYOND THE GALAXY.*
I LOVED THAT SHOW WHEN I WAS A KID! SO CLEVER OF THE FAIR TO DO A SKIT ABOUT IT.

HEY!

YOU KIDS DON'T HAVE PERMISSION TO DO THIS! WHAT'S GOING ON?

UH, A HOSTILE ALIEN!
CREW, RETREAT—
WAIT!

HOLD, MY GOOD SOLDIER. THESE STRANGERS HAVE CAUGHT THE EYE OF HER MAJESTY.

I GUESS
IT *IS* PART OF
THE FAIR.
SPORTS

YOUR MAJESTY,
I AM CAPTAIN FINN OF
THE *STARCRAFT
VIGILANCE*. THIS IS
MY LOYAL CREW.
DELIGHTFUL!
BUT HOW STRANGE
YOU LOOK TO US.
ARE YOU HUMAN?

I AM HUMAN, YOUR, UH,
QUEENLINESS, BUT SOME
OF MY CREW ARE FROM
BEYOND THE STARS.
WE ARE FROM THE
FUTURE—
CAPTAIN, WE
CAN'T MESS
WITH THE
TIME LINE.

OH, RIGHT! UM, WE ARE
EXPLORERS FROM...
UH, ANOTHER PART
OF EUROPE,
I GUESS?
THE
RENAISSANCE
WAS IN ITALY,
RIGHT?
MAN, I DON'T
KNOW! REMEMBER
THAT D MINUS I
GOT IN HISTORY
TWO WEEKS
AGO?

EXPLORERS! HOW AMUSING.
YOU MENTIONED YOU CAME HERE IN A STAR CRAFT? IS THAT SOME KIND OF FLYING MACHINE?

IT IS. A GREAT AND WONDROUS FLYING MACHINE.
I THOUGHT TO INVENT ONE OF THOSE MYSELF. ARE YOU AN INVENTOR, SIR?

NO, MY DEAR LEONARDO, THEY JUST SAID: THEY ARE EXPLORERS!
AH, YES. FORGIVE MY FORGETFULNESS, CAPTAIN.
THIS IS SO GREAT.

THERE IS NOTHING TO FORGIVE, SIR. BUT NOW WE MUST DEPART TO OUR SHIP.
SO SOON? HOW SAD!
I WISH YOU SAFE JOURNEY.

CLAP
DON'T FORGET TO WATCH *BEYOND THE GALAXY* SEASON FOUR, TONIGHT AT 8 P.M.!
CLAP CLAP
CLAP
FAREWELL, NEW FRIENDS!
CLAP CLAP
CLAP

YE OLDE
EMPLOYEE ENTRANCE
HAHAHAHAHAHAHA

HAHAHAHA
HAHAHA
HAHAHA

DID YOU GET IT?
GOT IT ALL.

NORRIE, YOUR COSTUME LOOKS SO GOOD!
I CAN'T BELIEVE I ACTUALLY FINISHED IT. I'M REALLY PRODUCTIVE WHEN I'M GROUNDED, I GUESS.

THIS IS WHEN THE FAIR ACTORS CAME IN.
YEAH, THOSE TWO ARE REALLY COOL. I LOVE WORKING WITH THEM.

YOU'RE AN AMAZING CAPTAIN FINN, SAM.
THANKS, LIEUTENANT NEKO.

WE'VE GOT TWO HOURS UNTIL THE PREMIERE. LET'S GET STOCKED UP ON SNACKS.
WE GOTTA PICK UP MY BROTHERS TOO.
CREW OF THE USS *VIGILANCE*, FOLLOW ME.

EVERYONE READY?
POP! CORN!
CHIPS!

READY.

CLICK!

AUTHOR'S NOTE

For most of my childhood and teenage years, I was a Horse Girl. I started taking riding lessons when I was very young, bouncing on a pony led around a ring by a teenage barn helper. My interest in horses exploded into a full-on craze as I got older, and everything became about horses. What kind of toys did I like? Horse toys. (My Little Pony and Breyer were my world.) What kind of books did I read? Books about horses. (The Saddle Club, Jean Slaughter Doty, and Monica Dickens were my favorites, and I combed the shelves of my local library, checking out any book with a horse on the cover.) What did I draw? Horses. (My very first comic, drawn in grade 1, was three panels about my mom buying me a horse.) I looked forward to my weekly riding lessons with an excitement normally reserved for Christmas morning.

Riding is an expensive sport. My parents were supportive of my interest in horses, but made it clear: If I was going to ride, I'd have to pay for it myself. I had a paper route, I babysat for family friends, and mucked out stalls at the barns I rode at. It was never quite enough to afford the horse lifestyle. I rode in jogging pants instead of riding breeches, rainboots instead of paddock boots, but I at least always had a helmet.

I desperately wanted my own horse. I kept lists of horse names in notebooks. What I'd name my horse if he was a chestnut quarter horse. What I'd name her if she was a dapple gray Arabian. But my paper route wouldn't pay for the cost of horse ownership, so I had to content myself with my weekly riding lessons. When I was a teenager, I was able to lease a lesson horse named Donovan for one glorious summer month. I spent every day that month at the stable with Donovan, imagining he was mine forever. After that summer, another girl took over his lease and I never rode him again.

Ride On is not a memoir, but it is inspired by my years as a Horse Girl. Some parts are true, like my childhood best friend getting her own horse and me being forbidden from riding it (though the resolution in the comic is more satisfying than what happened in real life, which is one of the best things about being an author). Most of the other parts of this comic are fiction. I spent more than a decade at horse barns, befriending the other Horse Girls (and the rare Horse Boy) who rode there. Outside the barn I had a hard time making friends, but Horse Girls, for the most part, were easy to get to know. We always had our love of horses to talk about.

Someday I'd like to ride again. I haven't ridden at all as an adult, which makes me a little sad. I imagine going back to the barn, smelling the heady aroma of horses. I see their long, beautiful faces, ears flicking back and forth, the feeling of their breath on my open palm. I'll return to the barn someday. For now, I dream of horses.

—FAITH ERIN HICKS

This photo is from my first year of high school, when I was taking a photography course (which is why the picture is black and white). I grew up in the era before smartphones, and my family's camera was a cranky manual that only my dad knew how to use. So, unfortunately, there are very few photos of me on horseback. The horse's name is Copper.

Published by First Second
First Second is an imprint of Roaring Brook Press,
a division of Holtzbrinck Publishing Holdings Limited Partnership
120 Broadway, New York, NY 10271
firstsecondbooks.com

Library of Congress Cataloging-in-Publication Data is available.

Our books may be purchased in bulk for promotional, educational, or business use.
Please contact your local bookseller or the Macmillan Corporate and Premium Sales Department
at (800) 221-7945 ext. 5442 or by email at MacmillanSpecialMarkets@macmillan.com.

First edition, 2022
Edited by Calista Brill and Kiara Valdez
Cover design by Kirk Benshoff
Interior book design by Molly Johanson
Color by Kelly Fitzpatrick

Drawn in Manga Studio 5 on a Wacom Cintiq, inked traditionally with a Raphael Kolinsky
watercolor brush and Koh I Noor ink on Bristol paper.

Printed in China by R.R. Donnelley Asia Printing Solutions Ltd.,
Dongguan City, Guangdong Province

ISBN 978-1-250-77282-4 (paperback)
1 3 5 7 9 10 8 6 4 2

ISBN 978-1-250-77281-7 (hardcover)
1 3 5 7 9 10 8 6 4 2